DISNEP
**Tangled**
The Series
...

TALES OF RAPUNZEL 1

# Secrets
# Unlocked

Simat

For Dana
—K.M.

randomhousekids.com

ISBN 978-0-7364-3826-1 (trade) —
ISBN 978-0-7364-3827-8 (lib. bdg.)

Printed in the United States of America

10 9 8 7 6 5 4 3 2 1

# DISNEY
## Tangled
### The Series

## TALES OF RAPUNZEL 1

# Secrets
# Unlocked

Adapted by
Kathy McCullough

Illustrated by
the Disney Storybook Art Team

Random House  New York

Long ago, in a kingdom called Corona, there lived a king and queen who eagerly awaited the birth of their first child. When the queen fell ill, the king ordered his guards to search for a cure. Finally, one was found: a golden flower that had grown from a single drop of sun. After drinking a broth made from the flower, the queen recovered and gave birth to a beautiful baby girl with hair the color of the sun. The king and queen named their daughter Rapunzel.

The kingdom rejoiced at Rapunzel's arrival—but before the baby was even a year old, she was taken. Her captor, an old crone named Mother Gothel, knew the flower's healing magic had been reborn in Rapunzel's blond hair. Part of its power was the ability to make someone eternally young. Mother Gothel wanted the magic all for herself.

Mother Gothel locked Rapunzel in a tower deep in the woods on the outskirts of Corona. The princess spent the next eighteen years there with only her pet chameleon, Pascal, for company. Then, one day, with the help of a thief named Flynn Rider, she escaped. Flynn cut Rapunzel's hair, destroying its power, and Mother Gothel instantly turned to dust. Rapunzel and Flynn—whose real name was Eugene Fitzherbert—fell in love, and Rapunzel

was finally reunited with her parents.

Rapunzel's hair, now short and brown, had lost its magic, but she no longer needed it. She was home safe, surrounded by loved ones, with a world of new experiences to explore. It seemed certain she would live happily ever after . . .

But as each new day brought new adventures, there was also the possibility of new dangers . . . and new mysteries.

On one such day, Rapunzel and Cassandra, Rapunzel's friend and lady-in-waiting, decided to venture beyond the walls of the kingdom to visit the spot where the magic golden flower had been found. A stone marker had been placed where the flower had grown, at the edge of a high cliff.

They arrived at twilight, and Rapunzel was

surprised to see spiky black rocks jutting up through the ground around the marker.

"They sprouted up about a year ago," Cassandra told her.

Curious, Rapunzel reached out toward one of the rocks. There was a sudden explosion of bright light, and new rocks burst up from the earth.

Rapunzel and Cassandra fled, but the rocks pursued them. More and more rocks appeared, each one larger and more threatening than the last.

As Rapunzel ran, her hair grew long again— as long as it had been before she left the tower. It also changed from its tawny brown to a golden yellow, the color of the sun.

Rapunzel didn't have time to react—she had to escape from the rocks. She and Cassandra ran as fast as they could, racing across the stone bridge that led back to the kingdom. Although the rocks tried to follow them, the bridge crumbled, and the vicious rocks were left behind.

But Rapunzel remained haunted by the memory of the sinister rocks, and by the many questions her encounter with them had raised. . . .

*R*apunzel's bare feet slapped against the marble floor as she chased Pascal down the wide hall of the castle. Her long blond hair, tied up in a braid, flew out behind her.

Pascal tried to blend in with one of the statues along the wall. His skin turned from green to gray to match the stone of the statue, but Rapunzel spotted him and he ran off.

Rapunzel and Pascal used to play hide-and-seek in the tower, but there hadn't been many places for either of them to hide. Now that they lived in a castle, there were endless places to hide.

There were dozens of halls and hundreds of rooms. There were passageways and tunnels. There were so many places to explore, Rapunzel still hadn't discovered them all.

Pascal slipped around a corner. Rapunzel followed him and spotted King Frederic and Queen Arianna talking to Eugene. Rapunzel paused to hug her parents and give Eugene a quick kiss on the cheek before hurrying off after Pascal, who had darted into a room at the end of the hall.

Rapunzel entered the room and noticed a cloaked figure standing at the far window. She felt a sudden chill.

The figure turned and lowered her hood. It was Mother Gothel! Her curly black hair seemed electrified. When she raised her arms, spiky black rocks suddenly sprouted in front of

10

her. The rocks tore up the floor, as if they were marching toward Rapunzel.

As the rocks got closer, Rapunzel's blond hair began to glow. Blinding light crackled between her hair and the rocks, causing her hair to come loose from its braid and fly around her in a shimmering golden swirl.

*"Your hair has returned!" Mother Gothel cooed in her silky voice. "Isn't it wonderful? Come now, dear. It's time to get you back to the tower, where you'll be safe." The rocks thundered closer.*

*Rapunzel was frozen in terror. She couldn't move. She couldn't speak. Everything went black as she heard Mother Gothel shriek, "Rapunzel!"*

Rapunzel's eyes snapped open and she jerked up in bed. Her blond hair flew up around her. She took a deep breath, calming herself, as her hair floated back down onto her shoulders like a protective blanket.

It was only a dream. She was in her room in the castle, safe and sound. Mother Gothel was dead and gone.

But the rocks . . . They were a new threat. Rapunzel once again recalled the night she had

first seen them, and how they had caused her short brown hair to grow long and blond again. She shivered, remembering how the rocks had chased her and Cassandra down from the cliff.

The rocks hadn't followed them to the castle, though. So why had they appeared in her dream?

It seemed to Rapunzel that the dream was a warning.

But *what* was it trying to warn her *about*?

"The dreams are trying to tell me some-thing, Cass," Rapunzel told Cassandra later that morning. They were in Rapunzel's bedroom, where Cassandra was braiding Rapunzel's hair. Pascal sat on a pillow on Rapunzel's nightstand and watched.

"Why were those rocks on the cliff?" Rapunzel continued. "Why did they cause my hair to grow back? Why did they chase us? Why—"

"*Shh, Raps!*" Cassandra whispered. She

glanced around, worried. "We can't tell anyone about that night."

Rapunzel lifted a lock of her long hair. "I think the secret is pretty much out, don't you?"

It had been impossible for Rapunzel to hide her newly long blond hair after they'd returned to the castle. There was too much of it!

She had finally confessed to her father about sneaking out, and had told him about the strange rocks. He forbade her to go beyond the walls of their kingdom again without his permission.

"We can't tell *anyone*," Cassandra repeated. "If your father finds out I helped you sneak out, he'll banish me from the kingdom!"

Cassandra had been adopted and raised by the captain of the royal guard, and she

was as skilled in sword-fighting as she was in braiding hair. It was her dream to one day get rid of the silk dress and veiled headpiece she had to wear as a lady-in-waiting and join the Corona royal guard herself.

"Don't worry," Rapunzel assured her. "I told my father I snuck out alone." She didn't plan to tell *anyone* the whole truth.

Well, except for the one person she *had* to tell.

"I have to tell Eugene what happened, though," she said.

"No, you don't," Cassandra insisted, placing a flower in Rapunzel's hair and tugging the braid tight. "As far as he knows, you woke up one morning with blond hair. That's all he *needs* to know."

"But he's my boyfriend!" Rapunzel protested. "We tell each other everything."

Cassandra was only a few years older than Rapunzel, but because Rapunzel had spent so much of her life cut off from the world, she seemed younger. She could be too trusting, thought Cassandra, wanting to see only the good in people. Cassandra, on the other hand, knew that even good people had flaws.

She stepped in front of Rapunzel and took her hands. "*Please*, Raps," she said. "Don't tell Eugene."

"Tell Eugene what?" Eugene bounced into the room, a coy smile on his face. "Are you two keeping secrets from me?"

Rapunzel looked from Eugene to Cassandra, torn. "Um . . ."

"Come on, Blondie," Eugene said, meeting Rapunzel's green eyes with his warm brown ones. "It's me, Eugene. You can trust *me*."

Eugene had helped Rapunzel find the confidence to leave the tower. He'd defended her from Mother Gothel and given up his life as a thief to stay with her in the castle. Didn't those things *prove* he was trustworthy?

"*I* don't trust you," Cassandra said before Rapunzel could reply. "You have a big mouth."

Eugene glared at her, offended. "Name one time I blew a secret," he demanded.

"When you told Queen Arianna what Raps had given her for her birthday *before* the queen opened her present," Cassandra said. "When you told me about my surprise party a week early. When—"

"I said *one*," Eugene snapped. "That's two already."

"I could go on, if you want," Cassandra replied. "And on, and on, and on . . ."

Eugene ignored her and turned to Rapunzel. "You're *really* not going to tell me?"

Rapunzel hated being caught between Eugene and Cassandra, two of her favorite people in the world. She trusted both of them with her life.

But with secrets . . . ?

"I'm sorry," Rapunzel said to Eugene.

"Fine," Eugene said. Rapunzel could see the

hurt in his eyes. "There are plenty of *other* people who trust me with their secrets—and I'm going to find some now." He marched out before Rapunzel could stop him.

Rapunzel turned to Cassandra. "Maybe we're being unfair to him," she said.

Cassandra shook her head. "Listen, we may be able to get some answers about your hair *ourselves*. Just the two of us."

"How?" Rapunzel asked.

"I know someone who might help. His name is Varian, and he's some kind of wizard."

Rapunzel perked up. "A real wizard?" She had never seen a wizard, but she'd read about them in books. "Do you think he'll have one of those pointy hats?" she asked, remembering the illustrations she'd seen. "And a robe and a staff? And cast spells and—"

22

"No, I don't." Cassandra grabbed Rapunzel's arms and looked her in the eyes, serious. "Very little is known about Varian, Raps. And what *is* known isn't good. Some say he's dangerous. Possibly even *deadly*."

Rapunzel thought it over. "But if we want answers, he's our best bet, right?"

Cassandra nodded.

"Well then," Rapunzel told her. "It looks like we've got a wizard to visit."

A few miles from the castle, at the edge of the forest, sat the Snuggly Duckling tavern. Eugene had spent a lot of time there when he was a thief and known by his alias, Flynn Rider.

"There they are!" Eugene called out to the patrons as he entered the tavern with Maximus, a horse and an official member of the royal guard. While Eugene and Max had once been enemies, they had bonded over their shared love for Rapunzel.

The pub was filled with the usual collection of thugs and hooligans. *My pals,* thought Eugene.

25

*Guys who would gladly share their secrets with me.* There was an old saying: "Honor among thieves." This meant that Eugene would surely find *someone* inside the tavern who trusted him.

He waited, but none of the men spoke up. "Come on! Doesn't *anyone* want to share anything with me? No secrets, no news—"

"I've got news," Hook Foot growled from under his seat. "You can't keep a secret."

Eugene frowned. He couldn't believe even *criminals* refused to trust him.

Just then, Big Nose entered the tavern holding a bouquet of flowers.

"Big Nose!" Eugene said to his friend. "Are those for your girlfriend? How are you two doing?"

"Glad you asked!" Big Nose replied. Eugene

26

smiled, pleased that Big Nose was willing to share something personal with him. "Perhaps this latest poem I wrote will answer your question."

The other thugs groaned.

After meeting Rapunzel, who had encouraged the thugs to follow their dreams, Big Nose had become a poet. But his poems could be epic—which means very, *very* long.

Big Nose unfolded a piece of paper. "It's called 'Can You Keep a Secret? I Love You,'" he said. He cleared his throat and began to read. "'Our love is like a timeless truth. It knows no tick nor tock. Our love is a big toe of honesty, poking through a hole in your favorite sock. . . .'"

Eugene could feel the other thugs glaring at him as Big Nose went on . . . and on and on. Max, bored, *clip-clop*ped over to the window.

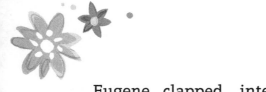

Eugene clapped, interrupting Big Nose. "Great poem! Thanks for sharing!"

"Sharing is what the poem's about!" Big Nose responded with a smile. "Because if you can't share everything with someone special, maybe that someone *isn't* so special."

These words struck Eugene hard. Did Rapunzel's refusal to trust him mean maybe he wasn't so special to *her*?

Eugene felt a tug on his collar as Max dragged him to the tavern window. Outside, they could see Rapunzel and Cassandra on another palace horse, Fidella, riding into the forest.

"Where are they going?" Eugene said to himself. It was another secret Rapunzel was keeping from him.

He decided to follow them. Whatever was going on . . . it wouldn't be a secret for long.

"So this is where Varian lives?" Rapunzel asked as she and Cassandra climbed down from Fidella. Pascal perched on her shoulder.

In front of them was a house. It sat atop a set of wide stone stairs and was tall and narrow.

"It seems cozy . . . ," Rapunzel continued. "In an 'I wish

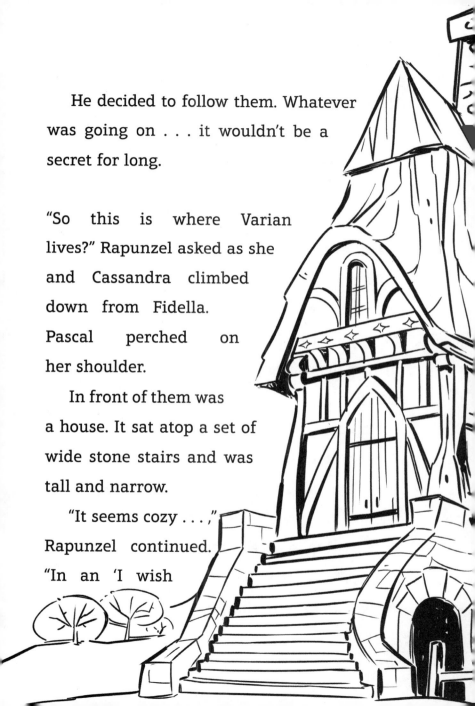

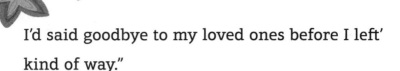

I'd said goodbye to my loved ones before I left' kind of way."

Cassandra tied Fidella to a post near an apple tree. She and Rapunzel each took in a brave breath and headed up the stairs to the house's entrance.

They entered together, stepping into a dark hallway. Ahead, eerie green light seeped around the edges of a closed door. Cassandra carefully pushed the door open, revealing a room filled with fog.

Rapunzel followed Cassandra inside. Neither of them saw the string stretching across the floor. Cassandra stepped on it, triggering a bottle of bubbling liquid on a shelf above them to tip over. The liquid oozed onto the floor.

*POOF!* Their feet were suddenly trapped in a sticky, bubble-gum-like goo.

A moment later, a hulking figure emerged from the fog. Red eyes glowed from the mask the figure wore over its face. "WHAT DO YOU WANT?" the figure boomed.

"We're, um, looking for Varian," Rapunzel said, her voice shaking. Pascal, clinging to her, hunched in fear.

"I . . . AM . . . VARIAN!"

He was unlike any wizard Rapunzel had seen in books. She swallowed her fear and gave him her friendliest smile. "Sorry to bother you, sir," she said. "We wanted to ask you about my hair, since you're a magic expert—"

"*MAGIC?*" Varian yelled. "I do not work with *magic!*" He lifted off his mask—revealing a short fourteen-year-old boy with shaggy brown hair, freckles, and a goofy grin.

Cassandra and Rapunzel stared in shock.

Varian wasn't a scary wizard; he was just a kid.

Varian leaped down from a stool to the floor. "I mean, *technically*, it isn't magic. It's *alchemy*."

Rapunzel knew that word. Alchemy was like chemistry. Alchemists were scientists who examined liquids, powders, and other substances to see what they were made of. They also mixed those things together to make new substances—like the goo trapping the girls' feet.

"You've just stepped in one of my latest creations," Varian said proudly. "See, we have a bit of a critter problem here." He waved to a raccoon stuck in the goo near Rapunzel and Cassandra. "I whipped up this mixture to trap the little guys without hurting them."

"Riveting," Cassandra said. "But could you get us *out* of here, please?"

"Oh, right." Varian searched his lab coat pockets. "Where did I put that neutralizing powder . . . ?" Finally, he pulled out what looked like a saltshaker and sprinkled some powder over their feet.

The sticky goo disappeared and the girls were freed. The raccoon darted off.

"Sorry about that, Your Highness," Varian said to Rapunzel.

Rapunzel stared at him in surprise. "You know who I am?"

"How could I not? I mean, look at your *hair!*" Varian gestured to the long golden braid hanging down Rapunzel's back.

"Please," she said. "Call me Rapunzel."

"*Really?*" Varian was amazed that he could call a princess by her first name. "Wow, okay. Anyway, everyone in the kingdom's heard

about your long hair coming back." He leaned down and whispered. "People say it's magic, but I don't believe it. As a man of science—"

"That's why we're here," Cassandra said, interrupting him. "Listen, kid, we need your help to figure out what the deal is with her hair, and what might explain why it came back." She stepped closer to Varian and stared down at him. "But whatever we find out, you've got to keep it a secret. You can't tell *anyone*."

Varian gulped. He could tell Cassandra was serious. He nodded.

Varian had Rapunzel lie down on a lab table. She'd unbraided her hair, and it streamed out from the top of her head to the end of the table and down to the floor.

He peered at Rapunzel's hair through a magnifying glass attached to a long metal rod. Varian pressed his lips together as he studied the blond strands. "It's very . . . long," he said finally.

Cassandra rolled her eyes.

"But don't worry," he continued. "I'm sure I can unlock the mystery of

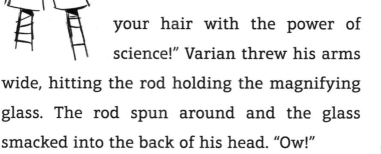

your hair with the power of science!" Varian threw his arms wide, hitting the rod holding the magnifying glass. The rod spun around and the glass smacked into the back of his head. "Ow!"

"Are you okay?" asked Rapunzel.

Varian patted his head with his hand. "Don't worry," he said. "It's just a little . . ."

He saw the blood on his hand. Suddenly, his eyes rolled back in his head and he collapsed to the floor.

Outside Varian's house, Eugene stood next to Max and Fidella at the apple tree. He'd been waiting for Rapunzel and Cassandra to come out for over an hour.

At first, Eugene had just been curious about what the girls were up to. Now he was getting worried. He no longer cared whether Rapunzel was keeping secrets from him. He just wanted her to be okay.

"I'm going in," he told the horses.

\* \* \*

Back inside the house, Varian sat across from Rapunzel. Part of her hair was wrapped around his head, covering the wound.

Cassandra stood nearby and watched as Rapunzel, with Pascal on her lap, sang the song Mother Gothel had taught her.

*"Bring back what once was mine,"* Rapunzel sang. The song had always caused her blond hair to glow and bring out its magical powers. She'd used that power to heal Eugene once, when he had cut his hand.

But her hair didn't glow this time. When Varian unwrapped it, the wound on his head was still there. "We've learned *one* thing about your hair," he said. "It no longer contains its legendary healing power." He smiled. "Progress!"

He leaped up and cracked his knuckles.

Varian's excitement at having a problem to solve made him forget his injury. "Now let's figure out exactly what that hair is made of!"

# CHAPTER 4

"Are you *sure* about this, Raps?" Cassandra asked.

Rapunzel, strapped to another lab table, gave her a thumbs-up. "Let's do this!" She was eager to see a real alchemist-wizard at work.

The table was connected to a larger machine and had been tilted up so it was perpendicular to the floor. Several odd-looking gizmos with sharp teeth, clawlike hooks, and pointed edges hung above Rapunzel's head. Pascal sat protectively on her shoulder.

"This machine can analyze any substance and determine its exact chemical makeup," Varian explained. He was now wearing gloves and a pair of goggles, in addition to his lab coat. "It should tell us all we need to know about your hair."

Wires led from the table to a control panel covered with gears and dials. Above the dials was a pair of levers, which Varian grabbed with both hands and pulled.

Suddenly, the table spun upside down, taking Rapunzel with it. "Whoa!" she cried.

Pascal leaped off Rapunzel's shoulder as the table continued to swing around. While Rapunzel rotated, the clawlike gizmos grabbed chunks of her hair, tugging it and stretching it every which way. Cassandra watched, worried.

Varian yanked the levers up and the machine stopped. "Done!" he announced.

"Okay, not super-fun . . . ," Rapunzel said, breathless. "But at least it's over."

"I meant done with the first test," Varian said. "Only eighty-six more to go!"

Behind him, a bell rang on a cuckoo clock–shaped counter atop a tall pole. Numbers on the front of the counter clicked down from eighty-seven to eighty-six.

The lab table slammed down and Rapunzel was once again parallel to the floor. A round saw lowered toward her hair, which now streamed out from the top of her head. Rapunzel's eyes

went wide as she realized the saw was going to cut through her hair.

Except it didn't.

Instead, it clanged against the blond strands and broke off from its arm, flying toward Varian—who ducked just in time.

"Amazing!" Varian shouted, delighted. "Your hair's absolutely unbreakable!"

"I'm betting *you're* not!" Eugene burst through the laboratory door. "Let her go!" he told Varian.

"Eugene!" Rapunzel cried. The machine had flipped her upright again, and its gizmos were tugging and twisting her hair. The counter clanged and clicked down with each new test.

Eugene was stunned to see Rapunzel smiling. "Blondie! You're okay."

"Hey!" Varian exclaimed. "You're Flynn

Rider!" He clapped his gloved hands together, thrilled.

Eugene's thief instincts went on alert. His first thought was *Deny everything*. "I don't know what you're talking about," he told Varian.

Varian dashed to a wall and drew back a curtain to reveal a Wanted poster of Flynn

Rider, surrounded by shelves filled with Flynn Rider adventure books.

They were the same books Eugene had read when he was young. He'd taken the name Flynn Rider from the books' hero, since his real name, Eugene Fitzherbert, wasn't very impressive for a thief.

The face on the Wanted poster was really him. The daring adventurer in the books wasn't.

"You're my hero!" Varian told Eugene. "I've read every single book about you." He held up one of the books. "Remember the time you dueled that evil knight blindfolded?"

"Well, see, kid," Eugene said, "that wasn't actually *me*."

Varian grabbed a cattle-prod-like device and waved it around like a sword. "How about when you fought the Earl of Camembert?"

Eugene held up his arms protectively. "Would someone please explain to me who this child is?"

"I'm Varian, master alchemist!" Varian declared. Suddenly, the ground rumbled beneath them.

"What was that trembling?" Eugene asked.

"Trembling? I didn't notice any trembling," Varian said, quickly changing the subject. "I just remembered I need my spectro-metric press to read the results of the tests." He leaned in toward Eugene and whispered, "If you come with me, Flynn Rider, I'll show you something special. But you've *got* to keep it a secret."

"Me?" Eugene asked. "You want to tell *me* a secret?"

Varian nodded.

Eugene grinned. "Let's go!" he said.

Varian left Cassandra to keep watch over Rapunzel and the hair-testing machine. Then he led Eugene around the outside of his house, to a shed cluttered with tools and machine parts.

Varian sifted through the mess. "Got it!" he said, lifting up what looked like a typewriter with wires hanging from the bottom.

Suddenly, the earth shook again.

"Why does that keep happening?" Eugene asked worriedly.

Varian set down the press and pulled up a

trapdoor in the floor of the shed. "Flynn Rider," he said, his voice low and important. "I believe I promised you . . . a *secret*."

He grabbed a lantern and climbed down the ladder inside the trapdoor, disappearing into the darkness below. Eugene reluctantly followed him to an underground pathway beneath the floor.

"These tunnels run through my entire village," Varian told him. "Which makes them perfect for my project."

"What project?" Eugene asked, although he was afraid to hear the answer.

"This project!"

At the end of the pathway, Varian held up his lantern, revealing a huge tank as big as his house. Pipes sprouted from the sides and top like tentacles. A smaller machine, with

dials and levers, was attached to one side of the tank. Clouds of steam puffed and swirled around the contraption.

Varian pointed to a vat of chemicals sitting near the tank. "Through the miracle of alchemy, I found a way to heat this entire tank of water with a single drop of my newest, yet-to-be-named compound." His eyes brightened. "I'll call it Flynnoleum!"

Eugene looked at the tank, confused. "I don't get it," he said.

"I'm going to surprise my village by bringing the people hot running water!" Varian explained. "I built a system of pipes that run—"

The tank shuddered, causing the ground to shake.

"Those tremors," Eugene said. "Is it your machines that are causing them?"

"My *machines* aren't causing them. The chemical reactions they *trigger* are," said Varian.

"Listen, kid," Eugene said. "Anything that causes earthquakes can't be safe. We've got to warn people about this."

"You promised you'd keep it a secret!" cried Varian. "Besides, I'm an expert. It's all perfectly safe. I've adjusted my calculations for every possible outcome. The margin of error is less than point five-six percent . . . or was it point five-seven?"

Suddenly, a bolt popped off the side of the tank and whizzed past Eugene. It pierced the tunnel wall, inches from his terrified face.

Eugene looked over at Varian.

Varian shrugged sheepishly. "I suppose I could turn it down a *little*."

# CHAPTER 6

While Varian stayed behind to recalibrate his hot-water tank, Eugene carried the spectro-metric press back to the laboratory.

The hair-testing machine was still spinning Rapunzel around while pulling her hair in every direction—and she was still enjoying it. "Only s-s-seven m-more t-tests t-to g-go!" she declared as the machine jolted her back and forth.

Eugene plugged the press into the control panel the way Varian had told him. As he did, there was another tremor.

"It's time to go," he told Rapunzel. "*Now.* Somewhere far, far away."

The numbers flipped from "07" to "06" as the counter clanged.

"We can't leave," Rapunzel protested. "We're almost finished!"

Cassandra looked at Eugene suspiciously. "Why do you want us to leave so bad?"

"Because when that thing blows—" Eugene caught himself. He was determined to keep Varian's secret. "Never mind."

"When *what* thing blows?" Cassandra demanded.

The counter clicked down to "05." *CLANG!*

Eugene glanced out the window. The ground was shaking all around them.

The counter clicked to "04," then "03."

"Okay, okay!" Eugene threw up his hands.

"I wanted to prove I could keep a secret, but I can't! Varian has—"

The floor shook again, the biggest tremor yet. Eugene and Cassandra were thrown off-balance. The pole holding the counter tilted and Pascal jumped to the floor as the numbers clicked to "02."

"Varian built this huge tank and some sort of heater underground," Eugene went on. "Both machines are clearly unstable. They could blow up *any minute.*"

*BOOM!* A loud explosion rattled the walls.

"And that minute is *now*," Eugene said.

Another *clang*—the counter flipped to "01."

Outside the window, chunks

of earth, gears, and machinery exploded from the ground and blasted into the sky.

"Get me out of this machine!" screamed Rapunzel.

Cassandra grabbed a wrench and banged at the contraption while Eugene tugged on Rapunzel's straps.

Varian ran past the window, still trying to fix things. "He's going to get himself killed," Eugene said.

"Get Rapunzel out of here!" Cassandra yelled to Eugene over the noise of the earthquake. "I'll get the kid!" She dashed out of the lab as Eugene struggled to free Rapunzel. The walls cracked around them. Chunks of the ceiling began to fall.

The counter flipped to "00." Just as the spectro-metric press started to spit out the results, a piece of the ceiling fell on the machine, crushing it. But Rapunzel was still trapped.

"You have to get out of here!" she told Eugene.

"No way," Eugene said, wrapping his arms around her. "I'm not going anywhere without you."

There was another rumble, and then another explosion. Eugene hugged Rapunzel tight. Pascal scurried under a blanket of Rapunzel's hair.

They all closed their eyes as the walls and ceiling collapsed on them.

Rapunzel could sense a warm light around

her and see a faint glow through her closed eyes. She waited for the rocks to crush them— but she didn't feel *anything*.

Suddenly, there was a burst of rocks exploding upward, followed by a clattering as the rubble fell to the ground.

Rapunzel slowly opened her eyes.

They were alive! Her hair had blossomed out around them like a giant canopy.

Eugene opened his eyes and looked up— and then at Rapunzel. "Did your hair . . . protect us?"

Rapunzel didn't have to say anything. She and Eugene both knew the answer was yes.

Cassandra and Varian were alive as well.

The explosions had propelled Varian's vat of Flynnoleum into the air, emptying its contents. As it flipped over and sped down toward him, Cassandra had run up to Varian and shielded him.

The open end of the vat had clamped down over them. Now they climbed out, shaken but unhurt.

Varian looked at Cassandra with awe. She had saved his life! "Thank you, milady," he said, gazing at her adoringly.

Cassandra rolled her eyes. Just what she needed—a would-be wizard with a crush on her.

"Varian!" a deep voice called out. A tall, broad-shouldered man ran toward them. It was Varian's father, Quirin. "Are you okay? What happened?" he asked. Quirin noticed

Varian's guilty expression. "Another one of your inventions?" he asked, gesturing to the rubble surrounding them.

"Sorry, Dad," Varian murmured.

Quirin frowned, disappointed. He turned away from his son and asked the assembled crowd if they were all right.

Cassandra left Varian with his father and ran off to check on Rapunzel. She was relieved to find the princess unharmed. Rapunzel explained how her hair had formed a magical shield to protect her, Eugene, and Pascal from the crumbling laboratory.

The girls agreed that the visit to Varian hadn't solved the mystery of Rapunzel's newly long blond hair. It had only raised more questions.

Thankfully, Max and Fidella were also

unharmed and they now stood by, ready to return everyone home.

But first, Rapunzel wanted to apologize to Eugene. "I'm so sorry," she told him. "From now on, no more secrets." She took a deep breath, ready to tell Eugene the truth—the *whole* truth. "You know how I said I just woke up with my hair long? I didn't. The night before that, Cass helped me break out of Corona."

"I knew it!" Eugene said. "She's going to get in *so* much trouble. . . ." Rapunzel gave him a warning look. "If anyone were to find out, that is," he added. "Which they won't. Because *this guy* can keep a secret." He pointed to his chest.

Rapunzel told him about going to the cliff where the golden flower had been found.

"There were these black rocks, and I know it sounds weird, but I think they're what made my hair grow back."

"After today, Rapunzel," Eugene said, "*nothing* sounds weird."

## The End

Tale Two

The

Great

Science Expo

Cassandra stood on a ladder in the castle courtyard, struggling to tie a giant banner between two poles. The banner read EXPOSITION OF THE SCIENCES.

"I don't see why the lady-in-waiting has to help set up for this thing," she grumbled to herself. "Who'd even come to a dumb science expo? Dorks, that's who."

"Who's ready for the expo?" an excited voice cried out from below. "Woo-hoo!"

Cassandra looked down to see Varian enter the courtyard pushing a cart. He was dressed

in his usual scientist getup: lab coat, rubber gloves, and a pair of goggles around his neck.

Cassandra and Rapunzel had met Varian when they'd visited him for help in figuring out why Rapunzel's long blond hair had grown back. Cassandra had heard Varian was a wise old wizard, but he turned out to be a teenage alchemist who liked to invent strange things— like the hot-water tank that had nearly blown them all up.

"Hey, Cassie," Varian said. "Want to see my new invention? It's a special device that can create an entirely new element, which I've named—"

"First off, it's Cass or Cassandra, not Cassie," Cassandra said. She knew Varian had had a crush on her ever since she'd saved his life in

the explosion at his house. A lovelorn alchemist was the last thing she needed in her life right now. "Second, I'm seriously behind on my chores, so—"

"Cassandra!" A castle guard named Stan ran toward her. "I thought you should know that the captain is short on guards for the expo today."

Cassandra scrambled down the ladder. Her father was the captain of the guard and had adopted her as a baby. He'd taught her all about fighting and defending the kingdom. It was her dream to become a member of the royal guard herself. Today could be her chance!

Cassandra leaped off the bottom rung of the ladder and grabbed Stan's arm. "Let's go!" she cried.

Varian watched her leave, disappointed.

"Hey, Cassandra! Looking good!" a voice called.

Varian turned to find Rapunzel staring at him through eyeglasses that looked like a pair of short telescopes.

"You should see some of the inventions on display," she said. "Look at these crazy goggles." Her magnified eyes squinted at Varian as she leaned closer. "Oh, hi, Varian! Sorry, I thought you were Cass." Rapunzel took off the glasses. "It's nice to see you!"

Varian's good mood returned. "I wouldn't have missed this expo for anything!" he said. "Wait until you see my invention!"

"Is this one deadly, too?" asked Eugene, who had arrived behind Rapunzel. Eugene had been

at Varian's house with Rapunzel and Cassandra when the hot-water tank had exploded.

"Ha, ha. No," Varian said. "I think you and everyone else at the expo will be *quite* impressed. Including Cassandra." He looked at Rapunzel with a hopeful expression. "She'll be there, right?"

"Of course," said Rapunzel. "I'm sure she doesn't have anything going on that is more important than *this*."

Stan and Cassandra hurried down the hall toward the captain's quarters. Cassandra hadn't had time to change out of her lady-in-waiting dress and into the tunic, tights, and boots she normally wore for guard training. This would have to do.

Stan opened the door and Cassandra snuck in just as her dad shouted, "We need more guards!" He was busy working out plans to patrol the big science expo. When he caught

sight of his daughter, he asked the nearby guards to leave the room.

"So, you want your first guard assignment?" he said to her. Cassandra nodded. The captain shook his head. "I just don't know whether you're ready."

"I've been training since I was six," Cassandra protested. "I know all the rules of guarding better than anyone. So if there's any reason why you feel I'm not ready—*besides* my being your daughter—I'm all ears."

The captain thought it over. He *did* need more guards for the expo. "Very well. But your lady-in-waiting duties come first. Only when you finish those may you help. Are we clear?"

Cassandra was thrilled. That was good enough for her. "Crystal clear!" she said.

\* \* \*

A corner of the courtyard had been blocked off as a reception area for the inventors and important guests to gather after the expo. It was Cassandra's job to set out flowers, juice, and pastries on the reception tables.

"There you are!" Varian called to her. "We didn't finish our conversation earlier! I was telling you about my invention. I really think you'll love it, but it takes two people to operate it. So how about being my assistant?"

Cassandra spun around to face him. "Assistant? No—*ah! No!*"

This last "no" wasn't to Varian. When she'd spun around, Cassandra had knocked over a pitcher of juice. A purple stain spread across the white tablecloth. "Noooo," she groaned.

"Allow me," said Varian. He took a tube of white crystals from his pocket and shook a

few onto the stain. Then he added water from a vase and the crystals exploded, sending out a purplish mist. The mist cleared . . . and the stain was gone!

"How did you do that?" asked Cassandra.

Varian held up the tube. "Rock salt. It mixed with the water from the flowers and the acid from the grape juice and absorbed the stain." He grinned. "Alchemy!"

Cassandra studied him, sensing that his science skills might come in handy with her chores. "Any chance you'd want to—"

"Help you? I'd love to!" Varian said. "And

then you can help me—and be my assistant! It'll only take a minute."

Cassandra thought it over. If she could get through her chores quickly, she'd save time, which meant she'd have at least a minute to spare to help out Varian.

"Deal," she told him.

As they went to work on her chores, Varian surprised Cassandra with his many useful inventions. He had a machine that polished eight spoons at once and a potion that could perk up droopy flowers in seconds.

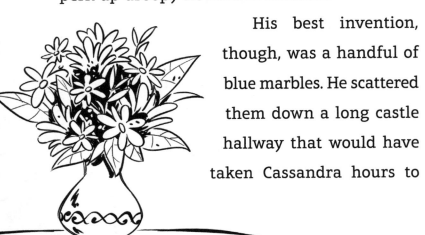

His best invention, though, was a handful of blue marbles. He scattered them down a long castle hallway that would have taken Cassandra hours to mop. The marbles foamed up, covering the stones in frothy soap. Then he tossed a yellow marble into the suds and—*POOF!* The suds disappeared, leaving the floor sparkling clean.

Despite Varian's help, by the time the clock tower bell tolled twelve, Cassandra was still only halfway through her chores. "There's no way I'll finish before the expo," she moaned.

"Why don't I finish your chores for you?" Varian suggested. "Then you can start your guard duty and we'll meet up later—and you can help me with my demonstration."

"You'd do that?" Cassandra asked.

"No problem," Varian said. "It's what friends do, right?"

Were they friends? Varian *had* helped her. A lot. What could it hurt to say yes?

"Right," she said. "Friends."

Tents had been placed around Corona's town square for the kingdom's inventors to show off their ideas before the official demonstration. Rapunzel dragged Eugene from one tent to the next, amazed by the objects on display. Eugene had brought popcorn along to munch on.

They stopped at one tent where a woman sat on a stool with pedals attached. The pedals were connected by a rod to a pitcher. When the woman pressed down on the pedals, the pitcher poured batter onto a griddle atop a

small cast-iron stove. The batter sizzled, and a few seconds later, a mechanical spatula flipped the flapjack to cook the other side.

"Wow!" declared Rapunzel. "That makes flipping flapjacks look like a piece of cake!" She grinned at Eugene. "Or should I say a *pancake*?" She giggled. Eugene smiled.

In the next tent, a farmer stood beside a wooden pen with two hoses running out from under it. One hose was attached to a pump, which the farmer pressed with his foot. This caused the hose to milk the goat inside the pen. The milk dripped through the other hose into a large pail. Suddenly, a head popped out from inside the milk pail.

"Shorty!" Eugene called out. Shorty was one of the pub thugs from the Snuggly Duckling, a tavern where Eugene had hung out back when

he was a thief. Shorty was the shortest and oldest of the thugs, and he tended to fall asleep in the oddest places.

Shorty sat in the milk and slurped it up through a straw. "Mmmm!" he declared.

Eugene spit out his popcorn, his appetite gone.

*KAPOW!* Colorful smoke exploded from the tent next door. Eugene and Rapunzel forgot about Shorty and the spoiled milk as a tall, pretty woman emerged from the smoke.

"Attention, science lovers!" the woman shouted. "I am the one, the only, Fernanda Pizzazzo!" She waved to a table covered with a velvet tarp. "What stupendimonious invention lies beneath this veil, you ask? You'll find out when master scientist Dr. Alcott St. Croix arrives to give *my* invention first prize!"

Rapunzel was wowed. The inventors were all so creative! She herself had painted pictures and built mobiles and baked cakes—but those were things that already existed. She had never made anything *new* like the things she had seen today.

Rapunzel turned to Eugene, her eyes bright with excitement. "I'm going to invent something, too," she declared, and ran off.

It didn't take Rapunzel long to come up with something to show Eugene. She remembered she'd *already* invented something, when she lived in the tower: a way to play catch by herself. She invited Eugene to her art studio to see it.

"I give you . . . the Hey-Hey!" Rapunzel announced, lifting a small wooden spool with

a long piece of string wrapped around it. She held the end of the string and threw the spool in front of her. The spool flew out as the string unwound, then returned to her hand as it rewound in the other direction.

"It *is* amazing, Blondie," Eugene told her. "But it's already been invented. It's called a yo-yo."

Rapunzel let the spool fall, disappointed. But she wasn't about to give up. "Luckily, I have another idea," she said, leading him across the room to a table covered with plates of vegetables.

"Carrots, celery, cucumbers," she said. "What do these foods have in common?"

"I don't eat them?" Eugene deadpanned. He was more of a popcorn and pretzels kind of guy.

"No! We chop them!" said Rapunzel. "But knives can be dangerous. That's why I invented . . ." She reached behind the table and lifted up what looked like a miniature guillotine. "The Safety Slicer!"

Eugene gulped. Regular-sized guillotines were used to chop the heads off criminals. Even though Rapunzel had painted the slicer pink and decorated it with flowers, the blade was still scarily sharp.

Rapunzel placed a carrot inside the hole under the blade while Pascal supervised from nearby. "Load it up and . . ." She dropped the blade, which cut neatly through the top of the carrot.

Eugene put his hand on his neck.

"It seems a little . . . extreme. Besides, I think they have something like that already, too."

Rapunzel frowned. It wasn't fair. She'd been locked in a tower for eighteen years! How could she possibly know everything that had ever been invented? Would she *ever* be able to come up with something new?

# CHAPTER 3

Cassandra and Pete stood in the hallway Varian had cleaned with his magic marbles. Cassandra had been happy with how shiny he'd gotten it—but she hadn't wanted to stare at it all day.

Her father had put her on "backup duty." That meant she had to stand at attention inside the castle and wait. She wouldn't be given any special duties unless she needed to replace another guard.

Even worse, she was *second* backup to Pete,

the first backup. At least she got to wear the official guard uniform.

Just then, the captain of the guard appeared at the end of the hallway with Stan. "You'll be Dr. St. Croix's personal guard," the captain told him. "It's probably the most important job of the day." Dr. St. Croix had been invited to the expo to judge the inventions.

"Thank you, Captain," said Stan. "I'm honored to—*ah!*" Stan's feet shot out in front of him and he crashed to the floor. "Ow!"

Cassandra spotted the puddle Stan had slipped in. It seemed Varian's marbles hadn't *completely* dried the floor.

The captain frowned and waved Pete over. "You'll need to replace Stan."

Pete, thrilled, dashed toward the captain. "Right away, Cap—*ah!*" Pete's foot hit the same

puddle and he crashed to the floor next to Stan.

Cassandra tried to hide her excitement—especially in front of the groaning guards. She glanced over at her father, hopeful.

"Are you up for this, Cassandra?" the captain asked. "You'll have to stay with the doctor during the whole expo. You won't be able to slip away—*even for one minute.*"

Just then, Varian passed by the end of the hallway, pushing a cart piled high with laundry. She'd promised to be his assistant—but she couldn't let this opportunity slip away!

Cassandra gazed up at the captain and saluted. "I'll do it," she said.

Cassandra met the doctor's carriage as it arrived in the castle courtyard. The carriage door opened and Dr. St. Croix stepped out.

"It's a pleasure to have you with us, Doctor," she said.

The doctor tugged on his velvet jacket importantly. "I imagine it would be," he replied, squinting down at her. "*You're* the personal guard I requested?" Cassandra nodded. Dr. St. Croix studied her, wary. "I expect you to be by my side *at all times*, do you understand?"

"Yes, sir."

Cassandra escorted the master scientist to the stage, where the judging for the expo would take place. An eager crowd had already gathered out front.

After King Frederic introduced Dr. St. Croix, the scientist gazed out at the crowd. "One of you will walk away with the greatest prize in all of science," he declared. "My approval! The rest of you . . ." He scrunched up his nose as

if smelling something bad. "May the universe show mercy on your pathetic souls!" he cried. The inventors exchanged nervous looks.

Dr. St. Croix marched to a podium at the side of the stage. Cassandra hurried to keep up with him.

"Let the judgment begin!" the doctor announced.

The curtain opened to show the first contestant: the farmer and his goat-milking machine. Dr. St. Croix watched as the farmer pressed the pump to milk the goat. "Can it milk a cow?" demanded the doctor.

"No, sir," the farmer answered.

Dr. St. Croix snorted, unimpressed. "Next!" he cried. The curtain closed.

*"Psst!"* Varian hissed to Cassandra from

the side of the stage. "You ready? A certain alchemist could use his assistant."

Onstage, the woman with the pancake-maker demonstrated her invention. "Next!" Dr. St. Croix called out.

Cassandra tiptoed over to Varian and whispered to him. "I'm sorry, but I can't help you anymore. I'm Dr. St. Croix's *personal*—"

"Hello!" Dr. St. Croix barked at her. "I told you to be by *my* side, not by the side of the stage."

"It's okay," Varian told Cassandra. "I'm sure I can find a new assistant . . . in the next five minutes."

Cassandra hurried back to Dr. St. Croix. She felt bad about letting Varian down, but she was sure he'd find another assistant.

At least, she hoped so. . . .

Big Nose, another pub thug from the Snuggly Duckling, stepped onstage and held up a spoon with a wooden handle. He flicked a trigger on the side of the handle and the spoon snapped down, replaced by a fork. He flicked the trigger again, and this time a knife snapped up. Big Nose repeated the action over and over—spoon, fork, knife.

"Next!" Dr. St. Croix shrieked. Big Nose pouted as the curtain closed in front of him.

A moment later, Rapunzel slipped from behind the curtain to the front of the stage.

"Dangerous, wet hallways!" she said to the crowd. "Cold, wet clothes! Hair that takes forever to dry!" She gestured to her long braided hair. "And I mean *forever.* Those things are *yesterday's* problems. Say hello to . . . the Mega-Dry!"

The curtain opened, revealing a giant fan on a large wheeled platform. Next to the fan, Max and Pascal stood on two treadmills—one big, one small.

"You guys ready?" Rapunzel asked her assistants. Max nodded. Pascal gave her a thumbs-up. Eugene grinned.

"You got this in the bag, Blondie," he said.

Rapunzel signaled to Eugene. He lifted a bucket of water—and dumped it over his head. Rapunzel waved to Max and Pascal, who began running on their treadmills, starting the fan. The blades of the fan spun faster and faster as the two animals ran, blowing a huge gust of wind through Eugene's hair.

"The Mega-Dry uses cutting-edge horse and chameleon technology to release a powerful, steady stream of air," Rapunzel shouted over the noise of the fan. "What used to take hours to dry now takes seconds!"

She signaled to Max and Pascal to stop

running. The fan slowed and Eugene ran a hand through his dry hair. A second later, his hair poufed out, making him look like a clown.

The crowd laughed. Eugene's cheeks turned pink and he pulled the empty bucket over his head.

"Oops," Rapunzel said. "I think I still had it set for *my* hair."

Dr. St. Croix rolled his eyes. "Next!" he cried.

The curtain closed on Rapunzel and her invention. She was disappointed—but at least she'd come up with something new!

Rapunzel spotted Varian waiting backstage, pacing nervously. She smiled and waved to him. So far the judge had hated all the inventions. But Varian had spent *years* inventing. If anyone could impress the doctor, it was him.

Varian stepped out from behind the closed curtain. "Behold!" he told the crowd. "The power of alchemy!" He waved to the curtain.

Nothing happened.

Varian coughed. A second later, Shorty appeared, stumbling as he pulled the curtain aside.

In the center of the stage stood a machine shaped like a large barrel. It sat on a bracket with its open end tilted forward.

"I give you . . . the Elemental Remogrifier!" announced Varian. He turned to Shorty.

103

"Assistant?" Shorty carried a bag of sand up a stepladder to the top of the machine. He poured the sand into the open end.

Varian gave a single turn to a crank on the side of the barrel and released the hand brake at the bottom. The barrel began to spin, faster and faster, until it was whirling at an incredible speed.

"The spinning heats up the sand," Varian explained, yelling over the loud rumble of the barrel. "The grains get pressed together, tighter and tighter, until they shrink down to . . . this."

Varian pulled the hand brake and the barrel stopped spinning. He reached in and drew out a small, sparkling crystal.

"I call it . . . Cassandrium!" he declared. The crowd burst into applause.

Cassandra watched from her post next to

Dr. St. Croix. She was stunned that Varian had named his invented jewel after her.

Meanwhile, Shorty, who had fallen asleep, tumbled off the back of the stage. He landed on the goat from the goat-milking machine, who kicked its legs out, hitting Big Nose. Big Nose threw up his hands, letting go of his fork/spoon/knife invention. It flew through the air—blade pointing out—headed straight toward the doctor.

Cassandra spotted a flashing glint of light as it reflected off the utensil. Her guard-training instincts kicked in, and she snatched the knife

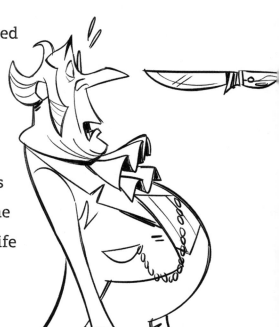

out of the air seconds before it hit Dr. St. Croix's nose.

The doctor quickly recovered from his shock and glared at Varian. "Despite its lack of dazzle, I was about to give your invention a 'so-so,' which is far above any other rating I've given today. However, since your assistant nearly got me killed, I'm afraid I have to disqualify you. Next!"

Varian stared at Dr. St. Croix, crushed.

"Excuse me, sir," Cassandra whispered to the doctor. "You can't disqualify him just because of his assistant—"

"You stick to guarding," Dr. St. Croix interrupted her. "*I'll* stick to judging."

Suddenly, a puff of purple and green smoke burst from the stage. The smoke

cleared, revealing Fernanda Pizzazzo next to a miniature cannon.

"This is the momensational moment you've all been waiting for!" Fernanda yelled to the crowd. "But first, I give you . . . chocolate!" She yanked a string attached to the cannon, which shot colorfully wrapped candies into the air.

Dr. St. Croix caught a candy and unwrapped it. "Now, *this* is science!" he said, popping the chocolate into his mouth. "Yum!"

Fernanda leaned down to the crowd. "Jaws, prepare to drop," she said. "Throats, prepare to scream. Eyes—take a good look around, because once I reveal my marveltacular creation, the world will never be the same again!"

She yanked the cover off the table behind her, revealing a strange-looking sculpture.

Two oblong stones about a foot tall each sat in a fancy iron base, with a smaller silvery orb between them.

"I give you . . . the Fantasphere!" She pulled a lever on the table and the oblong stones drew apart. The orb in the center rose as if by magic.

The crowd gasped, amazed. Varian, back in the audience, watched the round stone hover, confused. He knew the two stones at either end were just magnets. Pulling them apart caused the metal orb at the center to seem to float. It was a pretty simple trick, one he'd learned how to do by age four, using two toy magnets and an old nail.

"What does it *do*, though?" he called up to her.

"The real question is . . . what *doesn't* it do?" replied Fernanda, tossing a candy at him. "Now have a chocolate and be quiet."

Dr. St. Croix moved closer to inspect the device. "It's glorious!" he declared, his eyes sparkling. "I see no need to continue the contest. Nothing could possibly compare to this!"

He pinned a blue ribbon on Fernanda's

dress. She shrieked and raised her arms in victory. The crowd cheered.

Varian shook his head in dismay. Dazzle had defeated true science.

Cassandra watched, guilt-stricken, as Varian slunk off, disappearing into the crowd.

Cassandra led Dr. St. Croix to the reception area, where he was soon surrounded by fans and didn't notice when she slipped away.

She found Varian sitting at the edge of the courtyard, moping.

"You should have won," she said to him.

"I don't care about that," Varian said. "All I really wanted to do was impress you."

It was Cassandra's turn to be surprised.

"I thought if I showed you what I was capable of, you might see something in me,"

Varian continued. "Something special." He shrugged. "I was just being dumb."

"You *did* impress me," she told him. "You're a great kid. You're smart, kind . . . unique."

Varian smiled. "Thanks," he said.

Cassandra glanced to the side of the reception area, where all the inventions had been put on display. "It looks like Dr. St. Croix liked your invention after all."

Varian saw the doctor turning the crank on the side of his machine. He jumped up in alarm. "No, Doctor!" he shouted.

If the machine was turned too many times, it would build up too much pressure. It could . . . Varian didn't want to think about what could happen. He had to stop the doctor—if it wasn't already too late!

"You can't turn it that many times!" Varian yelled as he rushed up to Dr. St. Croix.

"Back off, young man," said the doctor, pushing him. "I am a scientist!" He released the hand brake and the barrel started spinning. It turned so fast, soon it was just a blur.

A second later, the barrel snapped free of its base and flew into the air. The crowd watched in shock as the barrel ricocheted off the courtyard walls.

"Somebody do something!" Dr. St. Croix cried as the barrel flew toward him and Varian.

Cassandra glanced from Varian to the doctor. She had time to save only one of them, and it was her duty to protect Dr. St. Croix. She ran forward—and grabbed Varian, pulling him to safety.

The barrel knocked into Dr. St. Croix, shoving him toward Fernanda Pizzazzo's magnet. As he flew in one direction, the barrel hit the magnet and flashes of light zapped between the three stones.

"Uh-oh," Varian said. "This is bad."

"How bad?" asked Cassandra.

Suddenly, the table with the magnets rose in the air, followed by the barrel. They whirled and swirled, creating a giant tornado.

"Unless we can stop it, its speed will keep increasing!" cried Varian. "It'll suck up everything in sight!" Objects were already

rising into the swirl:
flowers and tablecloths
from the reception area, then the tables
themselves.

"The only way to stop it is if I can
pull the hand brake," Varian said.
"But I have to get close—*ah!*" Varian
screamed as he was sucked into
the tornado. Cassandra grabbed his
ankle at the last minute and held on.

Varian raised his arm, but the hand brake was out of reach. "We need a powerful wind force to reverse it!" he yelled down to Cassandra.

Rapunzel had been watching from the edge of the courtyard. "The Mega-Dry!" she said to Eugene. He nodded, and they wheeled her invention from the display area toward the tornado.

Varian glanced down and saw Max and Pascal running on the treadmills. "No!" he yelled. "You need to *reverse* the direction of the wind."

"You have to run the other way," Rapunzel told the animals. Max and Pascal quickly turned around. The fans slowed and then sped up in the opposite direction, drawing air *in* instead of blowing it out.

The barrel lowered closer to Varian's hand. He grabbed the hand brake and pulled. The barrel came to a halt and the table with the magnets dropped to the ground. The barrel landed next to it.

Cassandra caught Varian as he fell, setting him down safely.

"Woo-hoo!" shouted Rapunzel. "We did it!" Max and Pascal stopped running. They huffed and puffed, out of breath.

"Hands down, your best invention yet, Blondie!" Eugene told Rapunzel. She smiled proudly.

Cassandra spotted Fernanda's blue ribbon on the ground and picked it up. "I believe this was meant for you," she said to Varian.

Varian smiled and took the ribbon. He reached into his pocket and lifted out the Cassandrium crystal, which he'd strung onto a necklace. "And I believe this was meant for you."

Cassandra put on the necklace. "Thanks, Varian. And I'm sorry about putting my job as a guard before our friendship."

The captain of the guard approached. "You helped prevent a possible disaster, Cassandra. Well done." Cassandra beamed. "As a reward, I have another job for you."

Cassandra didn't even wait to hear what the assignment was. "I'm sorry, Dad," she told her father. "Right now I need to do something more important—help my friend." She nodded to Varian, who was cleaning up the mess his machine had caused.

"Speaking as the captain of the guard, turning down an assignment doesn't bode well for you," he told her. "However . . ." He smiled. "As your dad, I'm proud of you."

Cassandra grinned and hurried to Varian and Rapunzel, who had joined in to help.

Varian had heard Cassandra's conversation with her father. "Wow," he said. "You turned down your dad for me?"

"I'll make it up to him," Cassandra told him. "It's not every day you get an element named after you."

Varian smiled. "I got the idea for creating it after seeing a cluster of strange black rocks by my village."

Rapunzel and Cassandra stopped working and exchanged a worried look.

"We need to see those rocks," Cassandra told him.

A few days later, Rapunzel and Cassandra met Varian at a hill behind his house. Shooting up from the ground was a gathering of the same kind of black rocks the girls had seen on the cliff where the magic golden flower had been found eighteen years earlier.

They were the same rocks that had caused Rapunzel's short brown hair to turn blond and grow long again. The same rocks had also chased Rapunzel until she and Cassandra

had gotten far enough away to escape.

They were the same black rocks Rapunzel still had nightmares about.

"They sprouted up a couple of weeks ago," Varian told the girls. "I've never seen anything like it."

Rapunzel took a step closer and her hair began to glow. The rocks glowed, too, casting a greenish light.

"Fascinating!" Varian declared. His keen scientific mind was spinning. "The rocks are demonstrating a physical response!" He pointed to Rapunzel. "To *you!*"

"Shh!" Rapunzel said quickly. "My dad's forbidden me to talk about the rocks to anyone. You need to promise to keep this between you, me, and Cassandra."

"You can count on me," he said.

Rapunzel smiled, relieved. "We'll figure out what the rocks mean together, *just us.*"

The three of them stared down at the rocks, which were still giving off their strange glow. As with her dreams, it seemed to Rapunzel that the rocks were trying to tell her something. . . .

## The End

Find out what happens next by reading more
## TALES OF RAPUNZEL
adventures!

Don't miss book #2:
## Opposites Attract